W9-AVK-492

M

For my little brother, Milo:
It's wonderful to share with you this life of ours. —S.B.

For baby Jennifer —B.W.

Little, Brown and Company

Hachette Book Group
237 Park Avenue, New York, NY 10017
Visit our website at www.lb-kids.com

Little, Brown and Company is a division of Hachette Book Group, Inc.
The Little, Brown name and logo are trademarks of Hachette Book Group, Inc.

First Edition: September 2010

Library of Congress Cataloging-in-Publication Data

Berger, Samantha.
Martha doesn't share! / by Samantha Berger ; illustrated by Bruce Whatley. — 1st ed.
p. cm.
Summary: Martha the otter learns there are unpleasant consequences for refusing to share with her baby brother.
ISBN 978-0-316-07367-7
International Edition ISBN 978-0316-12635-9
[1. Otters—Fiction. 2. Brothers and sisters—Fiction. 3. Sharing—Fiction. 4. Family life—Fiction.]
I. Whatley, Bruce, ill. II. Title. III. Title: Martha doesn't share!
PZ7.B452136Mard 2010
[E] — dc22
2009042678

10 9 8 7 6 5 4 3 2 1 SC Printed in China

The illustrations for this book were done in watercolor and colored pencil.
The text was set in Barbera, and the display type is Carl Beck.

Martha doesn't share!

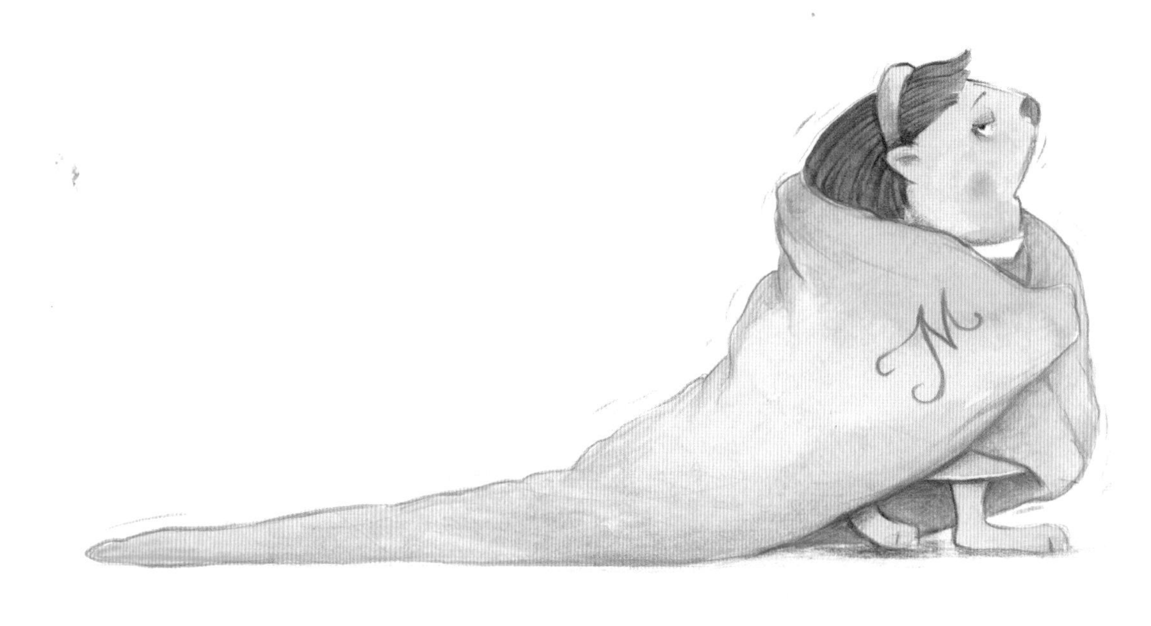

by Samantha Berger  illustrated by Bruce Whatley

Little, Brown and Company
New York Boston

Martha has a new favorite word,
and that word is . . .

Mine!

She says it about her pancakes.

She says it about her scooter.

She says it about her dollhouse.

She says it about her blanket, too.

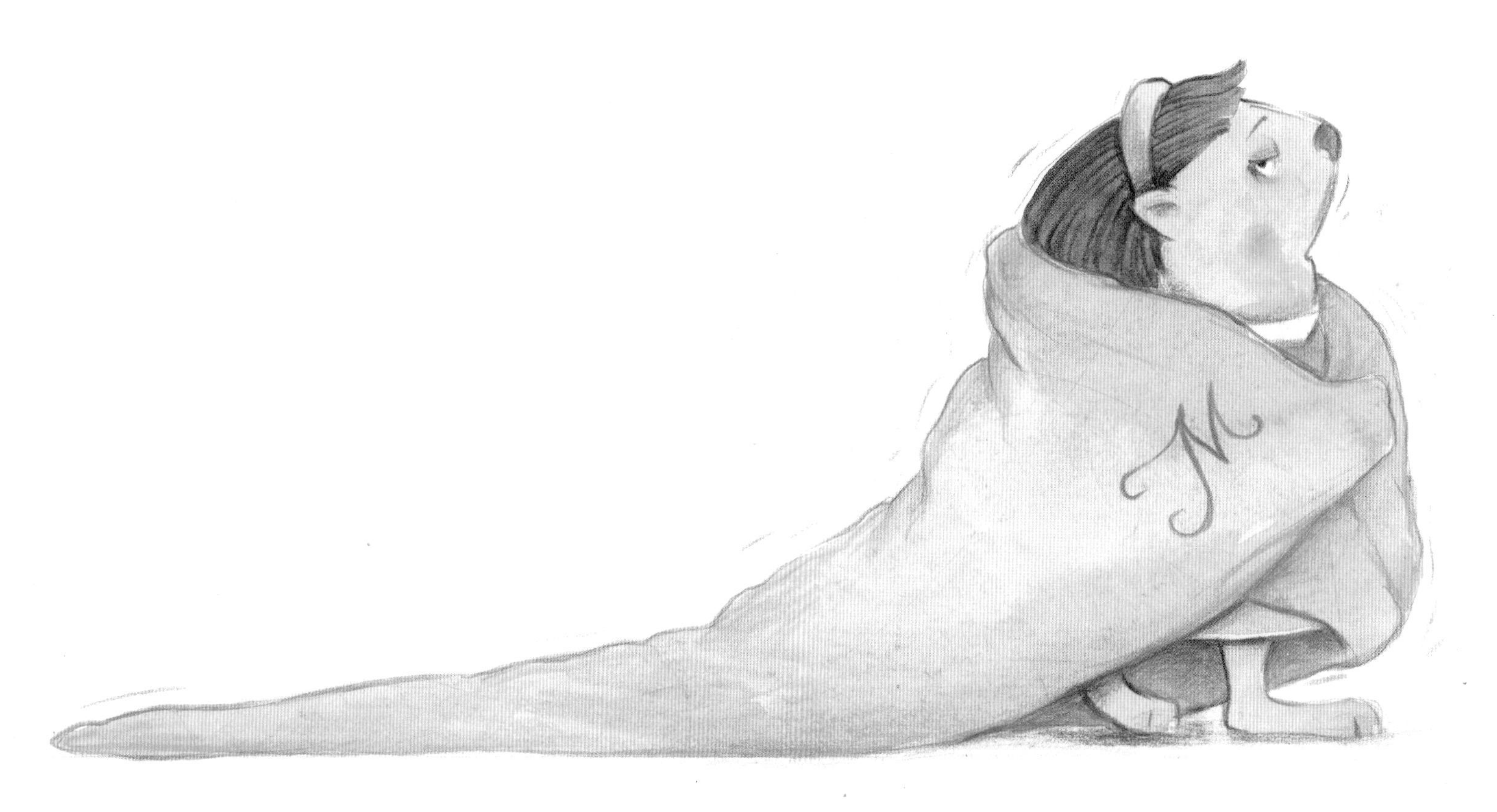

She says it about almost everything.

Mine.

Mine!

"Mye?" asks her baby brother, Edwin.

"No, *Mine!*" answers Martha.

Martha's parents would like Martha and Edwin to share.

"How about taking turns?" asks Martha's mother.

"You take a turn, and then Edwin takes a turn," says Martha's father.

But Martha doesn't like taking turns.

"Besides," she says. "It's *mine!*"

"Okay," says her mother
as she walks away.

"Okay," says her father
as he walks away.

"K, Maffa," says Edwin
as he waddles away.

Martha decides to put on her costumes.

But it's not nearly as much fun being a magician when you don't have an audience.

Martha decides to play with her puppets.

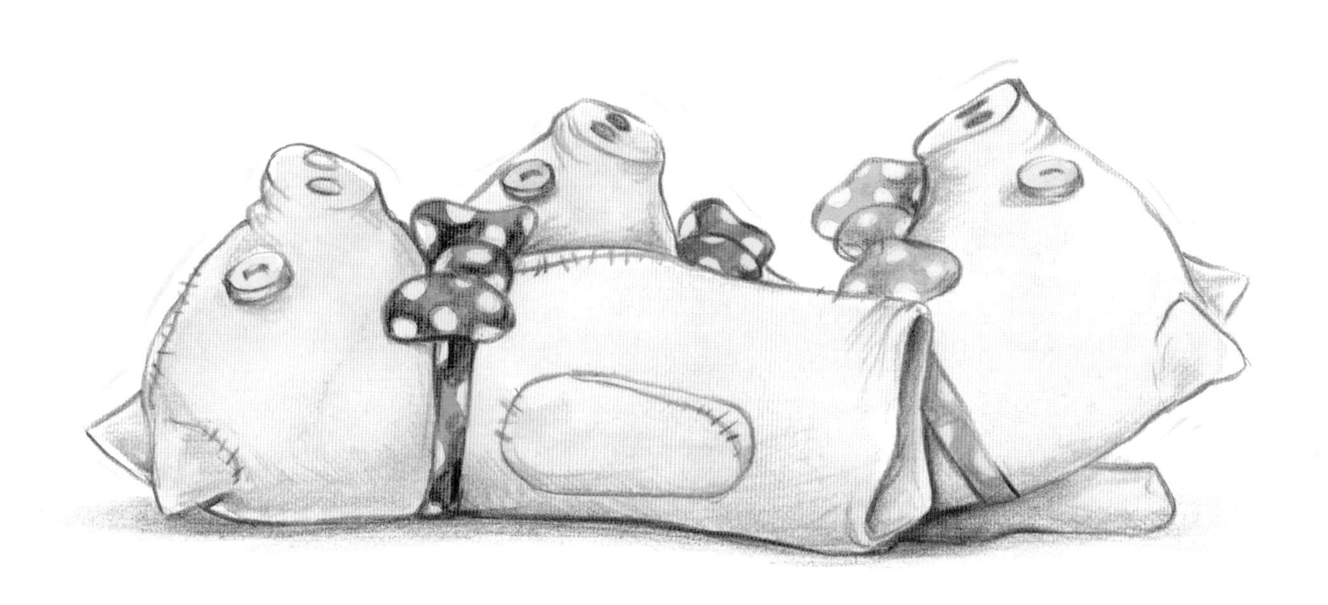

But it's kind of lonely being the wolf
when you don't have the three little pigs.

Martha decides to play a game.

But it's hard to ping
when you don't have someone to pong.

Martha thinks about sharing.
She thinks and thinks and thinks about it.

Then she thinks about it some more.

Martha decides to go find her family.

Roingy!
Roingy!
Roingy!

"Hi," says Martha quietly.
"Hi, Martha," says her mother.
"Hi, Martha," says her father.

Martha's baby brother, Edwin, stops bouncing and laughing. He looks at Martha and the things she brought with her.

"Edwin," says Martha,
" . . . could I bounce on your trampoline, too?"

Martha's mother looks at Edwin.
Martha's father looks at Edwin.

"Ya! Maffa, too!" shouts Edwin.

Martha takes a deep breath.
"Edwin," says Martha, "these are mine . . .
but you can play with them, too."

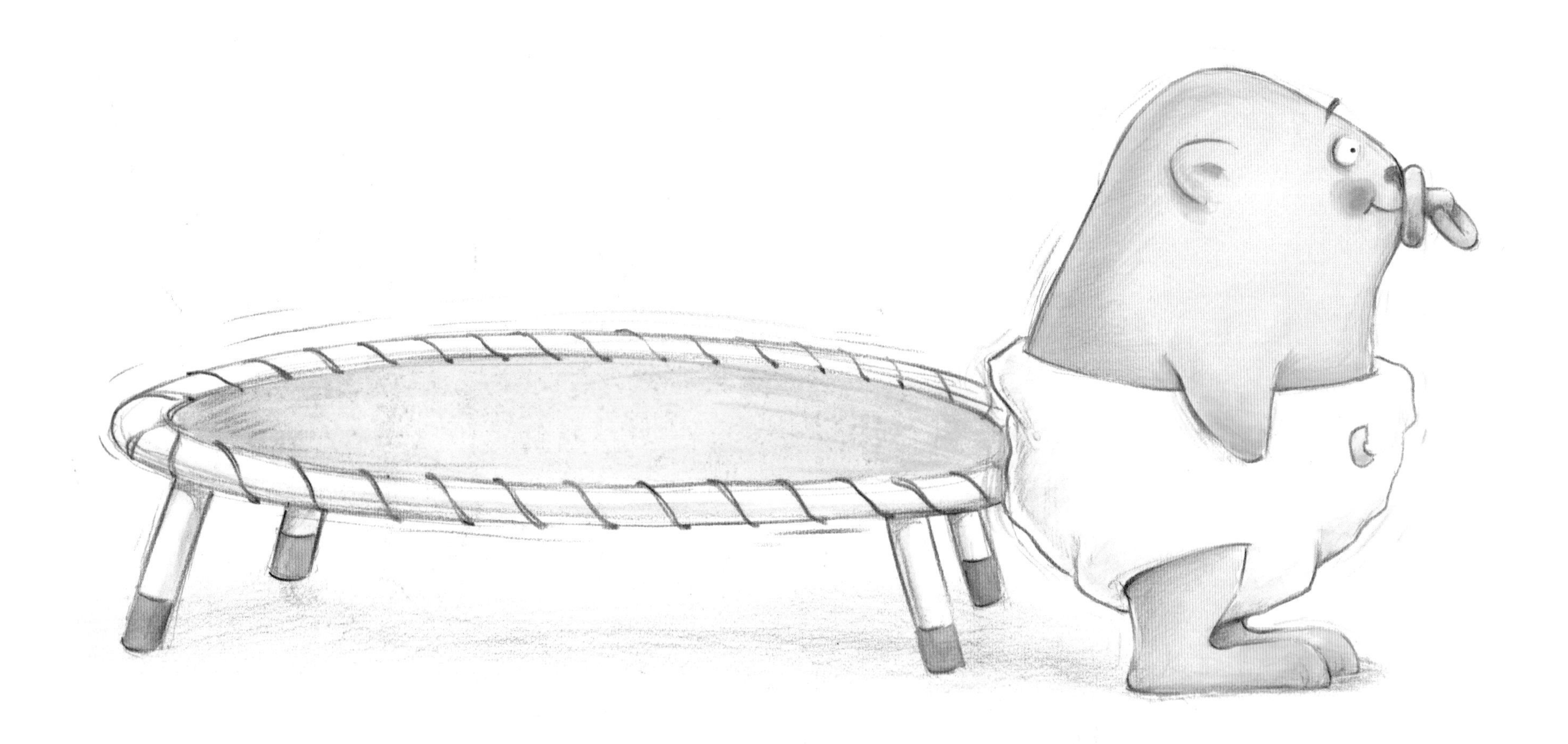

Edwin smiles at his big sister.
Martha smiles back at him.

Now, whenever she can, Martha tries to share with Edwin.

M

And she's getting better at it every day.

M